The Feather Club

by Beth Erlund

To Quinn,

Fly away to new adventures!

Erlund Johnson Studios
COLORADO ❖ FLORIDA

March 2011

I wish to thank my husband, **Dennis Johnson,** for his countless creative suggestions, his eye for detail and his never-ending support, my editors **Jessica Egan** and **April Lucas,** and my technical staff of **Greg Dunn** and **Karen McDiarmid.** Together they have made this second book of mine a success.

Inquiries about this book and prints of the batiks should be addressed to:
Erlund Johnson Studios
22528 Blue Jay Rd.
Morrison, Colorado 80465
(303) 697-5188
www.erlundjohnsonstudios.com

Printed and bound in Canada by Friesens of Altona, Manitoba

Erlund, Beth
The Feather Club / written by Beth Erlund
SUMMARY: The first migration experience of a young Canada goose
ISBN 13: 978-0-9762306-1-8
ISBN 10: 0-9762306-1-5
Library of Congress Control Number: 2007904186

For parents, grandparents and
role models everywhere who instill
self-confidence and a sense of
adventure in the young,
especially Virginia and Otheil Erlund
and Betty and Harry Johnson
who made us dare to dream
and seek adventure.

Tomorrow is the big day.

Tomorrow Ginny Goose will fly south
for the first time.

Winter is coming, the grass is turning
brown and the cold wind is
beginning to blow.

Tomorrow Ginny's mom and dad, her
sisters and brothers and
all her friends at the lake will
begin to fly south for the winter.

But tonight, Ginny is so excited she
can't fall asleep.

Tonight the moon is high in the sky
before Ginny tucks
her head under her wing and dreams
of flying south.

Today is the big day!

Today Ginny will fly south for the winter.

Ginny slowly opens her eyes.

Oh, no!

The sun is already high in the sky!
She overslept and everyone is gone.

Ginny's mom and dad, her sisters and brothers
and all her friends have flown.

Ginny is alone at the lake.

"How will I ever know which way to go?
Which way is south?" cries Ginny.

A little brown rabbit pops
up from the grass.
"I think you need to fly away from
where the cold wind blows.
I think south is where the cold wind
does not blow."

Excitedly, Ginny asks the rabbit,
"Do you go south for the winter?"

"No," says the little brown rabbit.
"I am a snowshoe hare
and my fur turns white like the snow.
I stay here for the winter.
You'd better start flying. Fly south now."

Ginny sees a grizzly bear
sunning himself near
the stream.

"Excuse me," asks Ginny,
"do you know how to go south
for the winter?"

The bear yawns.
"No, I don't go south for the winter.
I hibernate in my den all winter long.
Now I am getting very sleepy.
You'd better start flying away
from where the cold wind blows.
Fly south now."

At the end of the day,
Ginny settles in on the lake for the night,
feeling all alone.

As the sun rises the next day,
Ginny finds that she
is not alone anymore.

There is a duck, an old mallard duck
sitting nearby on the lake.

"Do you go south for the winter?" asks Ginny.

"I used to go south for the winter
but now I am so old. I think I will just stay here,"
says Max Mallard.

"Oh, please go south.
Please go south with me," begs Ginny.

As they talk about flying,
Max decides that the warm southern sun sounds good.

"Okay," says Max.
"I will show you the way to go south.
We will fly south together this year
if you don't fly too fast.
Follow me."

And so they do.
Two friends head south.

Late in the day, the two friends see a lot
of birds in a field down below.
Maybe they have
found Ginny's family.

No, these are really big birds.
One is standing off by himself.

As Ginny and Max bravely walk up to the very tall bird,
they ask, "Do you go south for the winter?"

With his head held high,
the sandhill crane looks down at them and says,
"Who are you and why are you asking?"

"I am Ginny Goose and this is Max Mallard.
We are flying south for the winter. Who are you?"

"You can call me Mr. Crane."

"Would you like to fly with us?" asks Ginny.

"My flock is very large and noisy," says Mr. Crane.
"I am ready to fly south soon. I think I will fly with you."

Ginny says, "We can be like a family as we
fly south together for the winter. We can be the Feather Club."

And so in the morning they do.
Three friends head south.

The Feather Club
flies and flies.

Winter is coming.
Soon it begins to snow.
Ginny, Max and Mr. Crane have to
stop to spend the night and wait
for the storm to pass.
They are cold and hungry.

When they land,
they come upon a little mouse.

Ginny says, "Please, could you help
us find a safe place to
spend the night?"

Matilda Mouse quickly leads
them to a sheltered spot where she
offers them some corn to eat.
They spend the night all
warm and cozy.

In the morning, Ginny says, "Thank you for your help.
Would you like to join the Feather Club and
fly south for the winter with us?"

Sadly, Matilda says,
"I wish that I could, but I can't fly. I am just a pocket mouse
and I have to stay here for the winter."

Together, Ginny, Max and Mr. Crane each give Matilda a feather.
"You are now an honorary member of the Feather Club."
So with promises of returning in the spring, the four friends part.
Matilda says, "Fly south now."

And so they do. Three friends fly south
and one friend settles into her new feather bed
to dream of flying south for the winter.

The Feather Club flies and flies.

When it is time to rest for the night
they see many lights ahead.
They decide it would be safer to stay
in the woods close by.

When they land,
a deer peers out of the brush.

"Those are the lights of people," he says.
"You don't want to get too close to them.
Not all of them like animals
from the woods.
It is better to spend the night
here in the woods with me."

And so they do.

The next morning,
The Feather Club
sees a very small bird quickly
flying from flower to flower.

"And who are you?" asks Ginny.

"I am Zippy Hummingbird,"
hums the small bird as she performs
loop-de-loops in the air.

"Do you fly south for the winter?" asks Mr. Crane.

"Oh yes I do. Yes I do, but the flowers here are
oh so sweet and almost good as new,"
hums Zippy.

Max says, "Why don't you come with us,
fly south now and be part of our Feather Club?"

"Just one more sip, just one more sip!" cries Zippy.

"Then we leave after breakfast," says Mr. Crane.

Soon, Ginny, Max, Mr. Crane and Zippy
say together, "We fly south now."

And so they do.
Four friends fly south.

As the sun rises the next morning,
a beautiful song awakens
the Feather Club.
They join in, adding their own individual voices.

Honk, Honk! Quack, Quack! Crank, Crank! Hum, Hum!

That morning, the woods are full of songs.

Hearing the Feather Club's music,
a little songbird says, "Who are you?"

Zippy answers, "We are the Feather Club and
we are flying south for the winter.
Would you like to join us?"

"Surely, I would. My name is Bobby Bluebird.
I was just singing my last goodbyes.
I am ready to fly south now with you."

And so they do.
Five friends fly south.

The Feather Club flies and flies.

When it is time to rest for the night,
they are all very tired.

But when they land,
they spy a coyote on the prowl
in the distance.

Max says, "That's a dangerous sight!
Any of us could be his dinner.
I think we need to move out onto
the pond for safety."

And so they do.
Five friends sleep and sleep.

They fly and fly. Soon Max knows they are getting close.

The prairie is spread out before them.
It is a wide expanse of dry grass full of little holes.
All of a sudden, a head pops out of
one of the holes.

"Hi!" squeaks Pete the Prairie Dog.

Another head pops up. "My name is Paul."

And another says, "I'm Pricilla."

"I'm Penny."

"I'm Pierre."

And on and on, there are many prairie dogs
looking out of their holes.

"Wow!" says Ginny. "There are a lot of you.
Do you go south for the winter?"

"No," says Pete. "We stay cuddled up under the
ground on cold days and on sunny days,
we warm ourselves up top. I guess you are
going south for the winter."

"Yes," says Ginny. "I hope we are almost there."

Pete smiles, "You will be there soon.
We see many birds flying by here on their way south."

That night the Feather Club sleeps and sleeps,
dreaming of tomorrow.

The next morning is full
of anticipation.
Ginny feels that today is the day.

The Feather Club flies and flies.

Soon, Ginny sees them below.
There are her mom, her dad,
her sisters and brothers
and her old friends from the lake.

They are all there! They honk,
"Hello, Hello!"

An old friend spies Max
and loudly quacks,
"Come down and rest your wings."

As they land, Mama Goose cries,
"Ginny, Ginny, I thought
you were lost. I am so happy to see you."
Then she looks more closely at the Feather Club
and says, "These are very funny geese
that are flying with you."

At that Max quacks,
"I am not a goose. I'm a mallard duck."

Mr. Crane cranks,
"I am not a goose. I'm a sandhill crane."

Zippy hums,
"I am not a goose.
I'm a broad-tailed hummingbird."

And Bobby chirps,
"I am not a goose. I'm a mountain bluebird."

Smiling, Mama Goose
thanks each one of them for helping
Ginny safely fly south.

It is time to say goodbye.
The five friends know
that Zippy and Bobby must fly further south.

Amidst the noise, Mr. Crane says,
"You know, my friends don't call me Mr. Crane.
My friends call me Sandy.
And you are now my very best friends."
With that, he hands each one a small feather.

Ginny, Max, Zippy and Bobby
offer their feathers in exchange as well.
They all promise to meet again in the spring
to fly north together.

The Feather Club waves goodbye
as Zippy and Bobby fly further south,
and Ginny, Max and Sandy
settle in for the winter.

She did it!

Ginny knows that her first migration south
has been a great success.

She has learned that friends can be

young or old,

large or small,

any shape or any color.

Ginny thinks this journey has been
the best adventure of her life.

She has learned that a friend is a friend forever.

Oh, and by the way, if you happen to see a bird fly by carrying some unusual feathers, you will know that it belongs to the Feather Club.

The End

CANADA GEESE mainly eat plants. Often during migration they will eat the leftover grains found in fields. Goslings (young geese) stay with their parents for the first year and then in the spring they fly back to their place of birth.

MALLARD DUCKS are called dabbling ducks because they feed on plants, bugs and even frogs while they are floating on top of the water. Sometimes they turn completely upside down in the water. Ducklings can swim as soon as they hatch but their mothers still provide waterproofing from the rain for their first summer.

SANDHILL CRANES will increase their body weight by as much as 18% as they prepare to migrate. They exhibit a lively dance, jumping high into the air when trying to impress a mate. They also "paint" themselves with mud and old grass to better hide them when nesting.

We usually think of **BROAD-TAILED HUMMINGBIRDS** as nectar eaters but they also catch small insects in flight. They are only four inches long and make tiny cup shaped nests out of woven plants, lichen and spider webs. The female throat is speckled white but the male has a brilliant red gorget.

MOUNTAIN BLUEBIRDS are not backyard birds since they like to eat insects, not seeds. In the fall and winter they will eat berries. They are known to hover over the grasses and catch insects in flight. Bluebirds usually can be heard singing at dawn.

SNOWSHOE HARES have very large feet that keep them from sinking into the snow when they hop or run. In the winter, they sleep underground in small dens and they come out to eat twigs and bark from trees and flower buds that stick up through the snow.

Even though **GRIZZLY BEARS** weigh between 400 and 1500 lbs, they can run up to 35 miles per hour. Normally a nocturnal, solitary animal, during salmon runs, many grizzlies will collect on the banks of the rivers to catch fish. They will gain several hundred pounds preparing for hibernation.

The **POCKET MOUSE** is small and because it has short hind legs it is not a good jumper. They store seeds in large cheek pouches. They do not really hibernate during the winter but sleep for long periods of time in their burrows.

Although often thought of as forest animals, **WHITE-TAILED DEER** also live on the prairie. After a year, the males start growing antlers which they will shed each December. They are able to make sounds that are unique to each individual and will warn each other of danger.

COYOTES have easily adapted to living around humans. Their name means "barking dog" and they are closely related to domestic dogs. They live in packs of many coyotes, but often will hunt alone. They eat small mammals, birds, insects and fish.

Relatives of squirrels and chipmunks, **PRAIRIE DOGS** are very social and live in "towns" with many acres of other prairie dogs. Their tunnels help the environment by preventing soil erosion. They have special color vision which helps them spot danger from far away. They call to each other by barking, using different sounds for each predator.

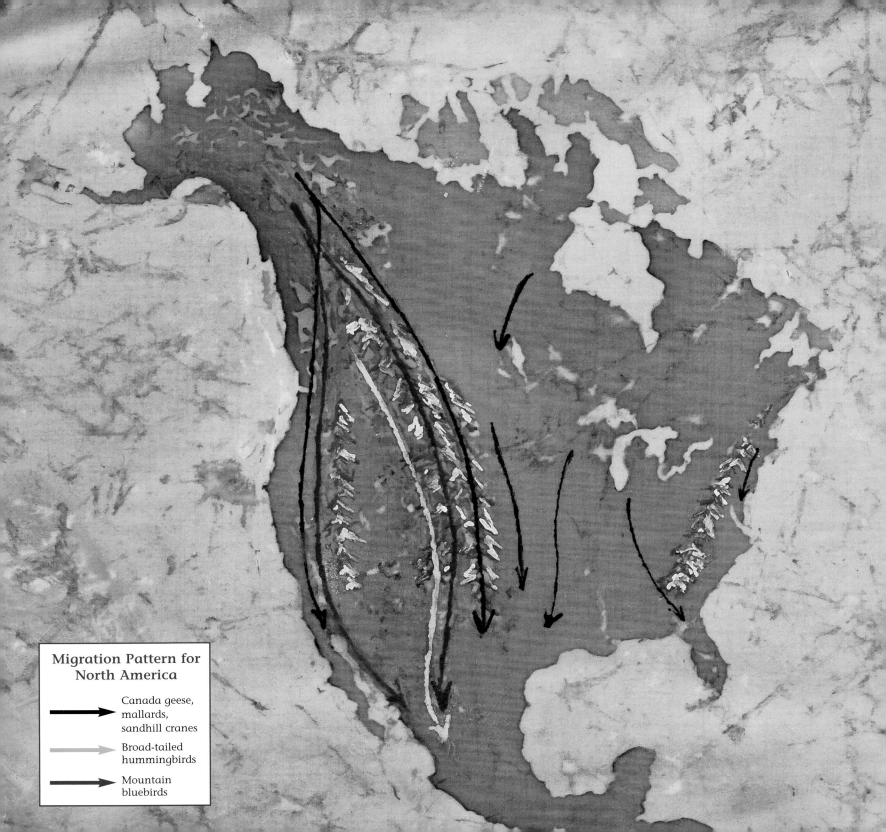

Migration Pattern for
North America

Canada geese,
mallards,
sandhill cranes

Broad-tailed
hummingbirds

Mountain
bluebirds

Batik: an art media using wax and dyes to make a picture on cloth. Over 2000 years ago, the Chinese used beeswax and resin to make designs to decorate the fabrics that they dyed. Today, batik is created by drawing a pencil sketch on cloth and then drawing with hot wax and paraffin. The portions that are to remain white are drawn first, then the lightest dye is applied.

When the cloth is dry, wax is again applied to the portions that are to remain the color of the cloth, and it is dyed again. This process is repeated thirty to fifty times to achieve details for each color. Finally, the wax is removed and the picture can be seen in the cloth. During the drawing process, the wax cracks and reveals little lines of color, adding the characteristic "crackle-look" that identifies the cloth as batik.

Encaustic: a mixture of beeswax, resin and pigments used to draw fine lines of texture atop a surface like batik. Heat is used to melt the mixture and fuse it to the surface.